THE PANAMA CANAL

BY

HARRY CLOW BOARDMAN

THESIS

FOR THE

DEGREE OF BACHELOR OF SCIENCE

IN

CIVIL ENGINEERING

COLLEGE OF ENGINEERING

UNIVERSITY OF ILLINOIS

PRESENTED JUNE, 1910

UNIVERSITY OF ILLINOIS
COLLEGE OF ENGINEERING.

June 1, 1910

This is to certify that the thesis of HARRY CLOW BOARDMAN entitled The Panama Canal is approved by me as meeting this part of the requirements for the degree of Bachelor of Science in Civil Engineering.

F. O. Dufour
Instructor in Charge.

Approved:

Ira O. Baker.
Professor of Civil Engineering.

OUTLINE OF THESIS ON THE PANAMA CANAL

		Page
I.	INTRODUCTION	v
II.	INTEROCEANIC CANALS	1
III.	HISTORY OF THE PANAMA CANAL	6
IV.	TYPE OF CANAL, (Lock or Sea-level)	13
V.	LOCATION, SIZE AND PLAN	20
VI.	ORGANIZATION OF FORCES	21
VII.	CONSTRUCTION OF THE CANAL PRISM	26
VIII.	CONSTRUCTION OF THE	29

LOCKS

IX.	CONSTRUCTION OF THE DAMS	33
X.	SANITATION	38
XI.	SOCIAL LIFE	40
XII.	ECONOMIC IMPORTANCE	43

I. INTRODUCTION

The building of a canal across the American Isthmus has occupied the attention of the world for four hundred years. While yet the sailors who crossed the sea with Columbus were living in all the vigor of mature manhood, a Spanish engineer drew the plans for an artificial waterway across the

Isthmus and submitted them to the King of Spain. From that time to this the building of an Isthmian Canal has been a fascinating project in the minds of progressive men. Attempts to build it have resulted in the loss of thousands of lives and the squandering of millions of treasure; and this "dream of the centuries" is still unrealized.

*PROPOSED ROUTES
FOR AN
ISTHMIAN CANAL.*

FIG. 1.

II. INTEROCEANIC CANALS

There are at least five routes which at one time or another have been chosen and seriously considered as possible locations for the Isthmian Canal. They are: the Atrato-Napipi, the San Blas, the Tehuantepec, the Nicaragua, and the Panama routes.

The Atrato-Napipi route follows the river Atrato, which empties into the Gulf of Darien, as far as the mouth of its tributary, the Napipi, thence up that river through the mountains and empties in Capica Bay. See Fig. 1, No. 1.

The San Blas route runs from the bay of the same name on the Atlantic side to the river Chipo which empties in the Gulf of Panama. It is only forty or fifty miles southeast of the Panama route. See Fig. 1, No. 2.

The Tehuantepec route begins at the bay of Coatzacoalcos in the Bay of Campeche and ends at the harbor of Salina Cruz in the Gulf of Tehuantepec. See Fig. 1, No. 3.

All modern engineers thrust these aside as impracticable, the first two because of the necessity for tunnels and the last because of its great length and number of locks. They will, therefore, receive no further attention.

The choice of the location for an Interoceanic canal has long been conceded by practical engineers to lie between the Nicaragua and Panama routes. A consideration of the natural advantages and disadvantages of these rival lines follows.

Since the Nicaragua route has been abandoned the features of the proposed construction will receive no attention. It is highly probable that this route would never have been seriously considered by the United States had it not been for the fact that the Panama line was for many years under the control of

France and apparently was destined to continue so for a considerable period.

Logically the question of harbors first suggests itself. Natural harbors do not exist in Nicaragua nor could one be excavated and maintained on the Atlantic side without a continual battle with forces which, in the last fifty years, have transformed what was once an excellent harbor at Greytown into a lagoon partially enclosed by an ever advancing line of sand brought down by the river San Juan. Experience on the South Atlantic and Gulf coasts of the United States has given abundant evidence of the results of a fight with such forces. In his "The American Isthmus and Interoceanic Canal" W. Henry Hunter says, "The policy which fights against the forces of nature is a mistaken one; it is foredoomed to failure. Nature may be aided in her operations; her more gigantic forces may to some extent be curbed and controlled; but an almost certain Nemesis pursues any effort which may be made to arrest and to determine in an absolute way a process so continuous as that of the filling up of the Greytown bight."

Brito, the Pacific terminus, is little better than Greytown since "even in the calmest weather there is a nearly constant surf, with breakers from four to ten feet high." Therefore, the terminus at Greytown would always be in danger of being filled up by the Atlantic waves and the one at Brito would constantly be liable to destruction by the Pacific breakers.

On the other hand the natural harbors of the Panama route have successfully met the demands of commerce for the last four hundred years. On the Pacific end practically no harbor improvements will be necessary. On the Atlantic the present needs are satisfied, but the large steamers of the future may require deepening which can be done and the resulting channel easily maintained since there is no persistent filling in process such as characterizes the Greytown harbor.

Volcanoes have long been plentiful in Central America, especially near the proposed Nicaragua canal. Nicaragua Lake, so geologists say, owes its separation from the Pacific to a great upheaval. There is now an active volcano near which ships would have to pass. From January 1, 1901 to April 30, 1904, a period of forty consecutive months, the instruments of the Instituto-Fisico Geografico, located 60 miles from the locks of the proposed canal, recorded 43 tremors, 91 slight shocks and 35 strong shocks, some of which lasted 16 minutes. Similar observations at Panama for the same period revealed only 6 tremors and 4 slight shocks, the longest being for a period of only 10 seconds. The lock gates of a canal might very easily be injured by earthquakes; and common sense would dictate that other things being equal, the canal should be placed where the shocks are fewest.

Strong trade winds rush through the San Juan gorge at all seasons. The rainfall near the Atlantic is enormous, averaging from 260 to 270 inches per year, and rain may be expected any day. In the western part the fall is only 65 inches, and there is also a well defined dry season. Clear vision is essential to safe passage through the canal and it is extremely doubtful if it could be obtained under the above conditions. Still more serious perhaps is the excessive curvature of the channel for 50 miles of its course. It is impossible to reduce the curvature to the limit which experience on the Suez canal has proved necessary for safety and speed. Furthermore the channel must carry off to the sea the drainage from 12,000 square miles of territory. This cannot do otherwise than create currents and eddies unfavorable to navigation.

The Panama route has no continued strong winds; the curvature is comparatively favorable; the annual rainfall is from 140 inches on the Atlantic coast to about 60 inches on the Pacific, with a definite dry season of three months; and the concensus of expert engineering opinion is that there need be no objectionable currents if proper provision is made for the regulation of the Chagres river. This phase will be discussed later as will also the question of curvature.

Much has been said about the advantages furnished by Lake Nicaragua which covers about 70 miles of the Canal route. However, for 29 miles of that distance, an artificial channel through soft mud would be necessary, and dredging would probably be practically continuous for maintenance.

From a purely engineering standpoint the most serious objection to this route is the liability to interruption for lack of water in seasons of extreme drought which are not at all uncommon in that region. Upon first thought it seems that a lake 3,000 square miles in extent cannot be other than an ideal source of supply, but such is not the case. By the proposed dam on the lower San Juan river the channel of the stream would become an arm of the lake through which all shipping would have to pass, the depth of water being, of course, dependent upon the lake level. This level has a natural variation of 13 feet. Under the projected conditions the whole outflow would pass over the dam about 50 miles away from the lake proper. The present high water mark cannot be exceeded without flooding valuable lands, nor, on the other hand, can the channel depth be made as great as desirable because the river bed is crossed by many rock ledges, and the cost of excavation fixes a limit to the depth economically practicable. The Isthmian Canal Commission of 1899–'01 concluded that the variation would have to be reduced to 7 feet. This means that the level would be held between 104 and 111 feet above tide water and the river bed excavated enough to give a minimum sailing depth of 40 feet. Records show no regular succession of high and low lake years; and as it is plainly impossible to keep a reserve sufficient to control such an enormous expanse of water, the regulation of this most important matter would be left to the judgment of the operator controlling the overflow at the dam. Carelessness or bad judgment on his part might therefore easily stop traffic for an indefinite period.

There is a similar question in regard to Gatun Lake of the Panama line although the majority of authorities anticipate no trouble from that source. A more complete discussion of this danger will be given later.

Concerning the actual difficulties of construction at Nicaragua, little need be said inasmuch as no work is now contemplated there. The San Juan dam of the Nicaragua and the Gatun dam of the Panama route both present conditions which have never been met before. Also the deep cuts of the Culebra find their counterpart in portions of the longer route.

The time-saving element is of more apparent than real importance because the time lost on the longer sea-voyage for the Panama route would be practically balanced by the gain of time in actual passage through the canal, the Nicaragua route being about four times as long as the Panama route. Henry L. Abbot, in his "Problems of the Panama Canal", estimates that 34 hours more time would be required for passage by way of the Nicaragua than by way of the Panama route.

An excellent reason for the adoption of the Panama rather than the Nicaragua route was the existence of a good railroad and the fact that the French had actually completed about two fifths of the work required.

SUMMARY OF COMPARISON

Below is given a summary of the comparisons which have just been discussed.

Panama Route	*Nicaragua Route*
There are two good harbors.	There are no good harbors.
There is a good railroad.	There is a very poor railroad.
Two-fifths of the work is completed.	No work is completed.
The projected construction, according to the majority of engineers, is justified by good engineering practice.	A dam without precedent in canal work is projected.
Except at Bohio, the annual rainfall nowhere exceeds 93	The most difficult works are where the rainfall is nearly

inches.	256 inches.
The length is 50 miles.	The length is 176 miles.
There are no active volcanoes.	There is one active volcano near the route.
The time of transit is 14 hours.	The time of transit is 44 hours.
The curvature is comparatively gentle.	The curvature is sharp.
No troublesome winds and cross-currents are expected.	Heavy trade winds and strong currents would be troublesome.

III. HISTORY OF THE PANAMA ROUTE

The Panama route as a line of transit was first established between the years 1517 and 1520. The first settlement on the site of old Panama, six or seven miles east of the present city, was made in 1517. The Atlantic end, called Nombre de Dios, was built in 1519. Here Balboa was tried and executed. It grew rapidly in importance and in 1521 became a city by royal decree.

Even at that early date a road was established across the Isthmus. It, however, did not enter the city of Panama, but at the Pacific end passed through a small town called Cruces on the Chagres river about 17 miles distant, and at the Atlantic end passed through Nombre de Dios. The latter terminus did not prove satisfactory so the town of Porto Bello was made the Atlantic Port in 1597. This also was subsequently abandoned. At least part of this road was paved, and bridges were built over the streams. Even today its course is well defined.

As early as 1534 boats began to pass up and down the Chagres river between Cruces and its mouth on the Caribbean shore and thence along the coast to Nombre de Dios, and later to Porto Bello. The commerce thus begun increased rapidly during the sixteenth century and Panama became a very important commercial center with a trade extending to the Spice Islands and the Asiatic coast. It was at the height of its power in 1585 and was called the "toll-gate between western Europe and Eastern Asia."

In time this commercial prosperity, which enriched Spain, called the attention of her rulers and others to the possibility of constructing an interoceanic ship-canal. Tradition says that Charles V ordered a survey in 1520 to determine the feasibility of a canal, but that the governor reported such an undertaking absolutely impossible for any monarch.

From that time the prosperity of Panama increased rapidly. Lines of trade were established with the west coast of South America and the Pacific ports of Central America. Its glory came to a sudden end when, on the sixth of February, 1671, it was sacked and burned by Morgan's buccaneers. A new city, the present Panama, was founded in 1673, but the old one was never rebuilt.

The project of a canal on this route, because of its romantic and commercial interest, was kept alive for more than three centuries without definite action being taken. Finally, in 1876, a French Company was organized at Paris to make surveys preparatory to building a ship canal across the Isthmus.

Lieutenant L. N. E. Wyse, a French naval officer, had immediate charge of the work. He obtained a concession, known as the Wyse Concession, from Colombia giving France the necessary rights for the construction of a canal.

In May, 1879, an international congress was convened in Paris under the auspices of Ferdinand de Lesseps, to consider the question of the best location and plan for the canal. This congress, after a two weeks session, decided in favor of a sea-level canal without locks to be located on the Panama route.

Immediately after this action the Panama Canal Company was organized under the general laws of France with Ferdinand de Lesseps as its president. The Wyse concession was purchased by the company, and after two attempts the stock was successfully floated in December, 1880. Two years were then devoted to surveys and preliminary work. In the plan first adopted the canal was to be 29.5 feet deep and 72 feet wide at the bottom. Leaving Colon, the canal passed through low ground to the valley of the Chagres river at Gatun; thence through the valley to Obispo where it left the river and crossed the continental divide by means of a tunnel and reached the Pacific through the valley of the Rio Grande. The tides on the Pacific were to be overcome by sloping the bottom of the Pacific end of the canal. No provision was made for controlling the Chagres.

Early in the eighties a tidal lock near the Pacific was added to the plan, and various schemes for the control of the Chagres were proposed, the one most favored being the construction of the dam at Gamboa. The tunnel idea was soon abandoned.

The French engineers estimated that the excavation would be about 157,000,000 cubic yards, that eight years would be required for completion, and that the cost would be $127,600,000. Work proceeded continuously until 1887, when a change to the lock type was made in order to secure the use of the canal as soon as possible, it being understood that the construction of a sea-level canal was not to be abandoned but merely deferred until financial conditions would allow its completion. This new plan placed the summit level above the Chagres river, and proposed to supply this summit level with water pumped from[8] that stream. Work went on until 1889 when the company became bankrupt; and on February 4, a liquidator was appointed to take charge of its affairs. Work was stopped on May 15, 1889.

The liquidator appointed a commission of eleven engineers to give him technical advice as to the condition of the work and the best methods for its completion. Five of these commissioners visited the Isthmus and reported on May 5, 1890. The report contained plans for the completion of a lock canal and emphasized the necessity for more complete examinations before beginning work. This advice was followed by the liquidator who at once took steps for the formation of a new company, and at the same time continued to take careful observations on the Isthmus, and these observations have been of great value since then.

The New Panama Canal Company was organized in October, 1894. It proposed to construct a sea-level canal from the Atlantic as far as Bohio (See Map, pp 45), where a dam was to form a lake as far as Bas Obispo, the difference in elevation being overcome by two locks. The summit level extended from Bas Obispo to Paraiso, and was reached by two more locks and received water from an artificial reservoir formed by a dam at Alhajuela in the upper Chagres valley. Four dams were located on the Pacific side, the two middle ones at Pedro Miguel combined in a flight.

Work continued on this plan up to the time of the Spanish-American War in 1898. About that time a "Comite Technique", as it was called, composed of seven French and seven foreign engineers who had been appointed by the Board of Directors of the New Company, submitted its final report upon the canal. It was estimated that, at a cost of $100,000,000 a canal suitable for all commercial needs could be completed in 10 years.

Had matters continued as before it is probable that the New Canal Company would have completed the canal as it had planned. But the Spanish-American War developed wholly new conditions. The trip of the Oregon around Cape Horn drew the attention of the American people to the importance of an interoceanic canal. Prior to this time the Board of Directors of the New Company, although aware that the Maratime Canal Company was actively engaged in securing funds from the United States Congress for the Nicaragua route, were so confident that a canal by that route could never seriously compete with their own that they gave little attention to the efforts of their rival. Now, however, if the newly awakened popular demand for a canal should induce the American government to undertake the work, the New Company would face two formidable conditions, namely, the difficulty of raising funds for the completion of the Panama Canal would be greatly increased if the parallel route were supported by the United States and the question of labor would become greatly complicated.

Knowing that the favorable conditions created by the French at Panama were unknown in the United States and certain that if known the United States would assist rather than retard the work the Board of Directors, on December 2, 1898, sent a complete copy of the report of the "Comite Technique" to President McKinley and offered to explain the exact conditions to any body of men appointed for the purpose. This offer came at the proper time since Congress was then ready to pass a bill to aid the Maratime Company in the construction of a canal on the Nicaragua route. On February 27, 1899 the representatives of the New Company were granted a hearing in the House of Representatives. They presented a technical exhibit, and stated that their company was authorized to reincorporate as an American company under American laws. So ably did they present their case that ultimately on March 3, 1899, by act of Congress a commission, known as the "Isthmian Canal Commission" was appointed by the President to determine the "most practicable and feasible route for an Isthmian canal, with the cost of constructing the same and placing it under the control, management, and ownership of the United States."

The original intention of the New Panama Canal Company in bringing the subject before the United States was not to sell its rights on the Isthmus but to reincorporate and receive the support of American wealth. However, it was evident that the United States desired absolute control, and accordingly the consent of Colombia to a transfer was obtained and the Company prepared a classified list of its properties which it placed before the Isthmian Canal Commission on October 2, 1901 with the statement that the sums given were not to be considered as final but were merely presented as a basis for discussion. The Commission, however, refused to take this view of the matter and persisted in considering the prices offered as constituting, when summed up, a definite lump sum for which the Company would sell its property. This lump sum was $109,141,500. The Commission's[10] valuation was $40,000,000. Consequently when the Commission made its final report it closed with these words, "Having in view the terms offered by the New Panama Canal Company this Commission is of the opinion that the most practicable and feasible route for an Isthmian Canal to be under the control, management, and ownership of the United States is that known as the Nicaragua route."

When the French Company heard this report it immediately offered to sell its property for $40,000,000. Accordingly the Commission made a supplementary report on January 18, 1902 stating that "After considering the changed conditions that now exist, the Commission is of the opinion that the most practicable and feasible route for an Isthmian canal to be under the control, management, and ownership of the United States is that known as the Panama route."

Thus it came about that the United States was authorized to obtain permanent possession of the concessions and properties of the New Panama Canal Company at a very low price.

Congress meanwhile had not waited for the report of the Commission but had passed a bill known as the Hepburn Bill, authorizing the President to acquire the right to construct a canal at Nicaragua and to begin the actual construction. Ten million dollars were appropriated and contracts for material and work to the sum of $140,000,000 authorized. Many discussions arose in the Senate; and a strong feeling in favor of the Panama route became apparent. Senator Hanna was especially active. He sent letters to eighty shipowners, shipmasters, officers and pilots, in which he enclosed a description of the two routes and a list of questions intended to bring out their relative merits from a practical viewpoint. Their answers were all in favor of the Panama route. As a result of the long debate a bill was passed June 26, 1902 with the President's approval. In effect it was as follows. The President is authorized to acquire for the sum of $40,000,000 or less the rights and property of the New Panama

Canal Company, and by treaty with Colombia, the perpetual control of the strip of territory necessary for operating the canal and is then instructed to proceed and complete the work under an Isthmian Canal Commission of seven members to be appointed by him. One hundred and forty-five million dollars was pledged for this purpose.

The Hay-Herran treaty with Colombia was signed January 22, 1902, but failed of ratification by Colombia. In November, 1903, however, there was a successful revolution upon the Isthmus and a republican form of government was adopted. The Hay-Bunan-Varilla treaty was thereupon made on November 18, 1903. It was ratified by both governments on February 26, 1904. It gave the United States control of a strip of land ten miles wide, five on each side of the canal.

Since then the work has proceeded under the complete control and supervision of the United States. The President, whose duty it was to provide for the government of the Canal Zone, put that as well as the engineering into the hands of the Commission of seven members which he had appointed. It has remained there. The office of chief engineer has been held by three men, J. F. Wallace, J. F. Stevens and G. W. Goethals, the first two of whom resigned.

The question of a sea-level canal was again agitated and became so insistent that the President appointed an international board of engineers, consisting of thirteen members, to assemble in

Washington September 1, 1905 to consider the various plans for the construction of the canal submitted to it. The board consisted of five foreign and five United States engineers, three of the latter having formerly served on the canal commission. The Board visited the Isthmus on September 28, had some examinations made for its enlightenment and in November submitted a majority report signed by the five foreign engineers and the three former members of the commission, and a minority report, the former advocating a sea-level canal and the latter a lock canal with the summit level 85' above the sea. The Isthmian Canal Commission with but one dissenting voice recommended the adoption of the lock type proposed by the minority.

On June 29, 1906 Congress in opposition to the majority report of the engineers, provided that the 85-foot lock type of canal be constructed across the Isthmus; and work has since continued on that plan. This final decision, however, was made with reluctance by many congressmen and some of them are regretting it today.

This Congress also decided that all materials used in building the canal should be purchased in the United States.

Early in 1909 a special body of engineers appointed by the President accompanied W. H. Taft on an inspection trip to Panama particularly with a view to determining the feasibility of the Gatun dam project. In a report made February 16 they unanimously approved the plans for the various changes in the original project made by the engineer. This included the widening of the locks to 110 feet and constructing the Pacific dams at Miraflores instead of at La Boca.

IV. TYPE OF CANAL

The controversy over the relative merits of a lock and a sea-level canal at Panama is as old as the question of building the canal itself. Supporters of the lock canal now in process of construction have sought to silence the storm of protest occasioned by its adoption; but in spite of their precautions reports have reached the American public which have created a lack of faith in the present engineers and their methods.

It is, of course, impossible for a layman to decide arbitrarily in favor of the lock or sea-level type. The only reasonable way to arrive at a conclusion is to examine carefully the arguments of both factions and reach a decision therefrom. The writer has found it difficult, if not impossible, to obtain an accurate presentation of the facts. Engineers high in their profession make contradictory statements. Presumably they honestly express their convictions but their failure to agree is strong evidence that there is a large element of uncertainty in the whole proposition. If they, acknowledged authorities, not only cannot arrive at a common decision in this matter, but consider it necessary to ridicule each other's plans, there is certainly cause to doubt the wisdom of the present project. It is the intention of the writer to state the principal arguments both for and against the two types of canals as presented by their most ardent advocates.

It is generally conceded that a lock canal at Panama would cost less than an efficient sea-level canal. Engineers on the Isthmus make an estimate of over $100,000,000 as the minimum excess of cost of a sea-level canal over the lock canal for construction alone. This estimate does not include the cost of carrying on the work of government and sanitation during the additional years which would be required to build a sea-level canal. Furthermore, it is true that there are many problems in connection with a sea-level canal, in spite of its apparent simplicity, which have never been solved and consequently no engineer can say how many millions would be required for its completion. Experience has shown, however, that the same unsolved problems were also true of the lock type. In their report to the President and to Congress, the minority of the board of consulting engineers pledged their professional reputations that if the lock type of canal were adopted the aggregate cost of completing the canal, exclusive of sanitation and zone government, would not exceed $139,705,200. Not four years have passed since that report was made yet $120,064,468.58 have already been appropriated and the great dams and locks are only fairly begun. In the last session of Congress it was proposed to increase the limit of the cost of construction of the Panama Canal to $500,000,000. Senator Teller in a speech said, "I have said again and again on the floor and I repeat it now — that if we get the canal built for $500,000,000, whether a lock or a sea-level canal, we shall do very well. In my judgment, we will never get that canal, in either form, except at a cost of more than $500,000,000." These figures are sufficient evidence that the engineers who made the original estimate were dealing with a subject too big for them.

At the time Congress voted to adopt a lock canal the estimated cost of a sea-level canal, excluding the cost of sanitation, civil government, the purchase price and interest on the investment (which seem unnecessary refinement in view of later developments) was given by the Board of Consulting Engineers as $247,021,000. The project on which this estimate was made provided for a waterway 40 feet deep at mean sea-level, 150 feet wide at the bottom in earth and 200 feet wide in rock, with a length of 49.14 miles. On the basis of this estimate advocates of the sea-level canal argue that on grounds of economy alone the lock type should be abandoned in favor of the sea-level type. It stands to reason, however, that some of the causes which have led to an increase in cost over the original estimates for the lock canal, such as the increase in the wage scale and the cost of material, and the adoption of the eight-hour day, would affect equally the sea-level project if it were undertaken.

The total estimated cost by the present canal commission for completing the work, including purchase price is $375,201,000, while the total estimated cost of the sea-level canal made by the same commission is $563,000,000. This latter sum is largely mere conjecture because of the many unknown elements entering into the problem; and there are successful engineers today who do not hesitate to state that a sea-level canal can be constructed for less than the present lock canal.

Very few question the statement that the sea-level canal would take longer for construction than a lock canal. The majority of the Board of Consulting Engineers estimated that from 10 to 13 years would be required. The Isthmian Canal Commission fixed the time at from 18 to 20 years and Lieutenant George W. Goethals, its chairman and chief engineer, states that the lock canal will be completed by January 1, 1915.

A great objection to the narrow sea-level canal is the difficulty of river control. The proposed plan was to construct a huge concrete dam 180 feet high across the Chagres at Gamboa. This of itself is a great undertaking but when done would not solve the question of flood control, for below Gamboa there are many more streams which if unregulated would plunge precipitately into the canal channel thereby not only creating cross-currents extremely unfavorable to navigation, and these would also erode the banks and settle deposits which would necessitate continual dredging for maintenance. If these rivers were not allowed to flow into the canal, the only other solution would be the construction of channels on either side of the canal to take care of this flow. This would be very expensive and decidedly dangerous since the rivers in places would be considerably above the canal. The old Chagres Channel and the old French diversion canal could be utilized for a part of the distance.

It is claimed that even a sea-level canal would require a lock at the Pacific end because of the enormous difference, sometimes 20' between high and low tides. Even the majority of the Board of Consulting Engineers, the supporters of the sea-level type, considered such a lock necessary. Since they made their report, however, a noted scientist, Dr. C. Lely, formerly minister of waterworks of Holland, has made an extended study of the question and states that the currents in a sea-level canal at Panama would not exceed those now common at Suez, namely, 2½ miles per hour.

On the other hand six huge locks are to be built on the lock canal, and they must be used at every passage of a boat. Their upkeep and operation will be a constant source of expense which would not exist in a sea-level canal. If one pair of locks is destroyed or put out of commission, the whole canal will be disabled and useless. Not only is this so, but they are a constant source of danger. The destruction of the gates of an upper lock, which is by no means an unknown occurrence, would allow the upper lake to empty into the canal channel, and probably destroy everything to the sea, including the dams. That such accidents can occur was demonstrated at the Welland Canal when a small steamer struck one gate and continuing her progress crashed through four other separate gates, the locks being 240 feet long. Again, at the Manchester Canal a vessel collided with a gate and carried it away, allowing the water to escape in such great volumes that it caused the other gates to give way also. Some conception of the force held in leash by the gates at Panama may be gained when it is stated that the "fall from the upper lock at Gatun to the empty second lock is over five times the rate of fall in the Whirlpool Rapids at Niagara and the depth is greater". It is true that various safety devices are to be installed at the locks but they can serve only to minimize not eliminate a danger which would not exist on a sea-level canal.

The curvature in the proposed sea-level canal is gentle, but for 19 miles of its course a large ship would continually be changing direction in a channel having a width of from one-fourth to one-fifth of her own length and in a current which may be as great as 5 feet per second. On the Manchester Canal all large vessels are aided by two tugs whose duty it is to help in steering. Through the above mentioned 19 miles speed could not exceed 6 miles an hour, and whenever a ship going the opposite direction passed, one or the other would have to stop and tie up to the shore as they do on the Suez Canal.

The courses on the lock canal are straight, giving a clear view ahead, and the vessels can pass without being forced to tie up. The great Gatun Lake will permit of full speed and in all ordinary cases in the passage from ocean to ocean enough time can be saved by reason of the wider and straighter channels of the lock canal to compensate for the time lost in passing through the locks.

While the question of flood control is solved by Gatun Lake the question of water supply is not. This lake must, under the present plans, furnish the water necessary for lockages. Experts have carefully studied this subject, and while most of them agree that there is water sufficient for immediate needs they also recognize the possibility of a scarcity in the future. General L. Abbot, one of the most enthusiastic supporters of the lock plan, states that there will be water for but 26 daily transits during the dry season which would accommodate from 30 to 40 million tons of annual traffic. Other prominent engineers [17] are not so sanguine and some go so far as to say the supply will be totally inadequate even for the first years of canal operation. At any rate there is a considerable element of uncertainty in the matter which actual trial alone will settle. No such trouble, of course, would exist in the operation of the sea-level canal.

Much has been said about the relative vulnerability of the two types. The arguments are decidedly at variance and approach the ridiculous when placed side by side. Common sense dictates that both types are open to injury by earthquakes or the hand of man; neither is invulnerable. It also seems evident that a lock canal with its many artificial devices is more open to serious injury by earthquake than a sea-level canal. In fact it is easy to believe that a shock severe enough to put a lock out of commission would scarcely affect a sea-level canal at all, and all who say otherwise are prejudiced. In fairness be it said that the danger from this source is exaggerated and probably should not occupy as large a place in the discussion of canal problems as has been given to it.

Lock canal advocates say a narrow sea-level canal could easily be obstructed by an obstacle placed in the channel; sea-level advocates say that a bag of dynamite under the lock-gates could put the canal out of service. Both statements are true but the essential element of difference is in degree. The obstruction in the channel would be no real injury to the canal at all: it would necessitate merely a few days work at the most for its removal. An injury to the locks, however, might readily mean draining of the summit lake and the destruction of all between it and the sea not to speak of the indefinite period required for reconstruction. The point is that it is practically impossible for man to seriously injure a sea-level canal; it is easily possible for him to so injure a lock canal. However, lock canals can be more readily defended in time of war because the points of attack are known beforehand.

A very serious objection to the lock type is that it cannot be readily enlarged. The locks are to be 1,000 feet long and 110 feet wide. This is ample for the present but indications are that future needs will be far greater. If they do become greater the Panama Canal will be an inefficient servant and will come far short of fulfilling the purpose which prompted its building. The sea-level canal could be enlarged by dredges without stopping traffic through it,[18] but with a lock canal it is different. When the locks as constructed become inadequate the only way to increase their capacity is to shut down the canal for years while new and larger ones are being built.

It is unquestionably true that the ideal canal is a sea-level canal 500 feet to 600 feet wide. This is of the type known as the "Straits of Panama" proposed by Philippi-Bunau-Varilla to the consulting board in 1905. There is a growing feeling that this plan is the one which will ultimately be adopted for the completion of the canal. It contemplates the construction of a lock canal to be finally converted into a sea-level canal. The locks were to be constructed so that as the levels were deepened by dredging they could be eliminated, navigation continuing during the enlargement. The material removed by the dredges was to be deposited in the lake formed by a dam at Gamboa. The plan was carefully considered and finally rejected because of the excessive time and cost involved. It is interesting to note what the author of the plans states in regard to it. He says in part, "It is easy to see from the records that this rejection was purely based on the false assumption that the transformation of rock into dredgable ground would cost $2.35 (per cubic yard), when it has since been officially demonstrated to cost eleven times less in the Suez Canal and eighteen times less in the Manchester Canal."

The cost at Panama of that transformation would be certainly inferior to the cost at Manchester not only on account of the saving of expense due to the gratuitous mechanical power given by the falls of the Chagres but also and principally on account of the extremely soft character of the greater part of the isthmian rocks. The electricity generated by the falls of the lake will put in action the rock breakers, the floating dredges, and the scows. The water in the small barge locks will raise the scows from the level of the summit to that of the lake and the depths of the lake will absorb the material of the straits. Thus the Chagres, once harnessed, will offer freely by its waters the way for the excavating and transporting instruments, by its falls the energy to animate everything and by its upper valley the dump to receive the spoils.

If unbiased and free-minded engineer officers of the army, having no anterior connection with the plans under discussion, should be sent to investigate the nature of the rock on the Isthmus and then to study in France, England, and Japan the actual improved methods of dredging soft and hard material the cloud would soon be dissipated. The supposed chimera would become a real tangible thing and the United States, the trustees of humanity in the construction of the great international waterway, would give to the world what it wants, what it is possible now and easy to obtain, the "Straits of Panama." This sounds very plausible; and it is a significant fact that engineers do not ridicule it. Their respect for it is growing. Today rock-dredging is on trial at Panama. If its feasibility can be there demonstrated the plan will undoubtedly be adopted.

No man can find objections to this type when once constructed. The objections to the narrow sea-level canal first considered do not apply to the "Straits of Panama", so they will stand as the ideal solution.

A canal designed to carry the world's commerce, to furnish free communication between the Atlantic and Pacific should be as free from artificial devices as it is possible to make it. It is therefore hoped that some day the present lock canal will be enlarged to an ideal, wide, sea-level channel.

V. LOCATION, SIZE, AND PLAN

The location, size and plan of the Panama Canal with several recent changes which have been ordered by the President and adopted by the commission is described in the "Canal Record" as follows: "A channel, 500 feet wide at sea-level will lead from deep water in Limon Bay to Gatun, a distance of 6.76 miles. At Gatun a dam one and one-half miles long and 115 feet high will impound the waters of the Chagres river in a lake, the normal level of which will be 85 feet above mean sea-level, A flight of three twin locks, each 1,000 feet long, 110 feet wide, and allowing for 41⅓ feet of water over the sills, will raise vessels from sea-level to the lake, or lower them from the lake to the sea-level channel. From Gatun navigation will be through the lake in a channel from 1,000 feet to 500 feet wide for a distance of 23.59 miles to Bas Obispo where Culebra cut begins. The channel through the continental divide, from Bas Obispo to Pedro Miguel, a distance of 8.11 miles will be 300 feet wide, and the surface of the water will be at the lake level. At Pedro Miguel vessels will be lowered from the 85-foot level to a small lake at 55 feet above sea-level, in twin locks of one flight. A channel 500 feet wide and 0.97 miles long will lead to Miraflores locks, where the descent to sea-level will be made in twin locks of two flights. The locks at Pedro Miguel and Miraflores will be of the same dimensions as those at Gatun. From Miraflores to deep water in Panama Bay, a distance of 8.31 miles, the channel will be

500 feet wide and 45 feet deep at mean tide. The channel widths given are all bottom widths. The entrance both in Limon Bay and in Panama Bay will be protected by breakwaters."

VI. ORGANIZATION OF FORCES

Work on the Isthmus is in the hands of an Isthmian Canal Commission, consisting of seven members, all of whom are appointed by the President. All of them have headquarters on the Isthmus. The present personnel of the Commission is as follows. Lieutenant Colonel G. Goethals, U. S. A., chairman and chief engineer; Major David Du B. Gaillard, U. S. A., corps of engineers; Major William L. Sibert, U. S. A., corps of engineers: Colonel William C. Gorgas, U. S. A., medical department; Harry Rosseau, U. S. A., civil engineer; Lieutenant Colonel H. F. Hodges, U. S. A., corps of engineers and Joseph C. S. Blackburn, civilian.

As chairman, Colonel Goethals receives a salary of $15,000 annually. Majors Gaillard and Sibert and

Civil Engineer Rosseau $14,000 each and Dr. Gorgas, Colonel Hodges and Mr. Blackburn $10,000 each.

The principal departments on the Isthmus, each in charge of a head who is directly responsible for the work carried on under his direction are: Construction and Engineering; Quartermaster's; Subsistence; Civil Administration; Sanitation; Disbursements; and Examination of Accounts.

The Department of Construction and Engineering is subdivided into the following named divisions; Atlantic Division from deep water to and including the Gatun locks and dams; the Central Division from Gatun to Pedro Miguel; and the Pacific Division from Pedro Miguel to the Pacific.

The Department of Construction and Engineering is under the direct charge of the Chief Engineer. The general plans come from the office of the Chief Engineer and details are left to division engineers, subject to his approval. The whole idea of the organization in this department is to place and fix responsibility, leaving to each subordinate the carrying out of the particular work intrusted to his charge. The Chief Engineer is assisted by the Assistant Chief Engineer, who considers and reports upon all engineering questions submitted for final action. The Assistant Chief Engineers have charge of the designs of the locks, dams, and spillways, and the supervision of these particular parts of the work. There is also attached to the Chief Engineer an assistant who looks after mechanical forces on the

Isthmus, and has supervision over the machine shops, the cost-keeping branch of the work, the apportionment of appropriations, and the preparation of the estimates. There is also an assistant engineer, who has charge of all general surveys, meteorological observations, and river hydraulics.

The Quartermaster's Department has charge of the recruiting of labor, the care, repair, and maintenance of quarters, the collection and disposal of garbage and refuse, the issue of furniture, and the delivery of distilled water and commissary supplies to the houses of employees and the construction of all new buildings. Operating in conjunction with the purchasing department in the United States, the Quartermaster's Department secures all supplies needed for construction and other purposes, and makes purchases of material on the Isthmus when required.

The common labor force of the Commission and Panama Railroad is more than 25,000 men, and consists of about 6,000 Spaniards, with a few Italians, the remainder being from the West Indies. The Spaniard is the best worker, although he objects to working in water. The total number on the pay rolls will average more than 30,000. Of these 5,000 are "gold men", that is, officials, clerks and skilled laborers, all of whom are American recruited through the Washington office. In the month of September, 1909, there were approximately 44,000 employees on the Isthmus on the rolls of the Commission and the Panama Railroad. There were actually at work, on November 3, 1909, 35,311 men, 27,672 for the Commission and 7,639 for the Panama Railroad Company. The salaries and wages of these men are paid once a month.

This Quartermaster's Department also has charge of the property records, receives semiannual returns of property from all those to whom property has been issued, and checks the returns and inventories of the storehouses with the records compiled from the original invoices.

The Subsistence Department has charge of the commissaries and the manufacturing plants which consist of an ice and cold-storage establishment, a bread, pie, and cake bakery, a coffee roasting outfit, and a laundry. These belong to the Panama Railroad Company, as, at the time they were established, money received from sales could be reapplied, whereas if operated by the Commission it would have reverted to the Treasury, necessitating reappropriation[23] before the proceeds of the sale could be utilized. They are, however, under the management of the subsistence officer of the Commission, who has charge of the various hotels, kitchens and messes.

There are 16 hotels from Cristobal to Panama which serve meals to the American, or "gold" employees at 30 cents per meal. There are 24 messes where meals to European laborers are served, the cost per day being 40 cents; and there are 24 kitchens for meals supplied to the "silver" laborers (men paid in Panamanian currency), the cost to the laborer being 30 cents per day. There is no profit to the Commission. The commissaries and manufacturing plants are operated at a profit so as to repay the Panama Railroad Company for its outlay in six years from January 1, 1909, at 4 per cent interest.

The Subsistence Department also has charge of a large hotel at Ancon for the entertainment of the Commission's employees at a comparatively low rate, and of transient guests at rates usually charged at first class hotels.

The Department of Civil Administration exercises supervision over the courts, which consist of three circuit and five district: the judges of the three former constitute the supreme court. The district courts take cognizance of all cases where the fine does not exceed $100 or imprisonment does not exceed 30 days. Jury trials are restricted to crimes involving the death penalty or life imprisonment.

The Sanitation Department looks after the health interests of the employees. It is subdivided into the health department, which has charge of the hospitals, supervision of health matters in Panama and Colon and of the Quarantine, and into the sanitary inspection department, which looks after the destruction of the mosquito by various methods, as grass and brush cutting, the draining of swamp areas, and by oiling unavoidable pools and stagnant streams.

To this Department also belong 11 chaplains employed by the Commission to attend the sick as well as look after the spiritual welfare of the employees.

All moneys are handled by the Disbursement Department, which pays accounts which have been previously passed upon by the Examiner of Accounts.

The Examiner of Accounts makes the examination required by law prior to the final audit of the accounts by the Auditor for the War Department. The pay rolls are prepared from time books kept by foremen, timekeepers, or field clerks, subsequently checked by the Examiner of Accounts who maintains a force of inspectors. The time inspectors visit each gang, generally daily, at unknown times to the foreman, time-keeper, or field clerk, and check the time books with the gangs of workmen; the inspectors report to the Examiner of Accounts the results of their inspection not in connection with timekeeping but all violations of the regulations of the Commission that may come under their observation.

Payments of pay rolls are made in cash, beginning on the 12th of each month and consuming four days for the entire force on the Isthmus.

The last published financial report of this Department was as follows:

Statement of Receipts, Disbursements, and Balances Available to June 30, 1909.

Receipts

Appropriations by Congress	$176,432,468.58
Rentals collected and returned to appropriations	264,393.76
Collections account sale government property, etc.	4,235,141.50
Balance due individuals and companies, account collections from employees	1,856.73
Total receipts	180,933,860.57

Disbursements

Classified expenditures		106,795,058.38
Department of civil administration	$2,932,951.06	
Sanitary department	8,741,715.40	
Hospitals and asylums	$4,656,125.99	

Sanitation	4,085,589.41	
Department of construction and engineering		54,832,540.14
Canal construction	48,311,622.16	
Municipal improvement on Zone	4,245,913.98	
Municipal improvements in Panama and Colon	2,275,004.00	
Cost of plant		40,287,851.78
Rights of way and franchises		49,107,914.89
Rights acquired from the Republic of Panama	10,000,000.00	
Rights acquired from New Panama Canal Company	39,107,914.89	
Payment to	40,000,00	

New Panama Canal Company	0.00	
Less value of French material sold or used in construction	892,085.11	
Panama Railroad Company stock purchased		157,118.24
Loans to Panama Railroad Company for reequipment and redemption of bonds		4,009,596.03
Paid into United States Treasury for sale of government property, etc.		3,572,141.50
Services rendered and material sold individuals and companies		2,764,001.30
Unclassified expenditures		4,877,072.36
Material and supplies	4,813,158.37	
Other unclassified items	63,913.99	
Advances to laborers for their transportation		48,783.26

Bills collectible outstanding		517,585.79
Total		171,849,271.75
Less amounts included in above but unpaid on June 30		1,694,355.70
Salaries and wages unpaid on rolls to June 1, 1909	181,291.08	
Pay rolls for the month of June, 1909	1,513,064.62	
Net disbursements		170,154,916.05
Balances available June 30, 1909		10,778,944.52
Congressional appropriations	10,114,087.79	
Miscellaneous receipts of United States funds	663,000.00	
Collections from employees account individual and companies	1,856.73	
Total		180,933,860.57

Note. — By an act of March 4, 1909, additional

appropriations were made to continue the construction of the Isthmian Canal, during the fiscal year 1910, available for expenditures July 1, 1909, as follows:

Expenses in the United States	$225,000.00
Construction and engineering	27,388,000.00
Civil administration	630,000.00
Sanitation and hospitals	1,915,000.00
Reequipment Panama Railroad	700,000.00
Relocation of Panama Railroad	1,980,000.00
Sanitation in cities of Panama and Colon	800,000.00
Total	33,638,000.00

VII. CONSTRUCTION OF THE CANAL PRISM

Excavation throughout the whole length of the canal is being carried on as much as possible in the dry as this has been found to be the cheaper method.

Upon the Atlantic Division, during the fiscal year 1908–'09, a dredging fleet consisting of one sea-going suction dredge, two 5-yard dipper dredges and three French ladder dredges worked on the section between Mindi and deep water, removing 6,039,934 cubic yards, of which 427,005 cubic yards were rock. The rock is removed by blasting. Holes averaging 15 feet apart are drilled to a depth of 50 feet below sea level, loaded with dynamite and fired. At the close of the year nearly 3 miles of the channel from deep water were completed.

The plans for breakwaters in Limon Bay were recently changed. Originally breakwaters were planned to extend nearly parallel to the axis of the channel to protect against filling by wave action. However, it was found that the northers entering between these breakwaters would lack room to dissipate and so vessels would be unprotected for a great portion of the distance to the locks. Accordingly two breakwaters have been planned which are to be so placed as not only to prevent filling but also to give shelter to shipping.

On the Culebra section of the Central Division considerable trouble has been caused by the great rainfall. To carry the rain off quickly diversion channels have been constructed at a large expense of money and labor.

Water falling in the prism is cared for by the cut itself. In the process of deepening pilot cuts are started from either end towards the summit which is now between Empire and Culebra. Drainage in either direction is by gravity through these cuts.

The total amount excavated from the canal prism in this division during the past year was 18,442,624 cubic yards, 12,291,472 cubic yards being rock. At the close of the year 43,574,954 cubic yards remained to be removed. The material is loaded on the cars by steam shovels, is hauled to the various dumps, and unloaded by a huge plow-like apparatus which is drawn from end to end of the train. Part of the spoil aided in the rebuilding of the Panama Railroad; the rock from Empire and Bas Obispo went to Gatun for the dam, and some material was hauled to Balboa on the Pacific and was there used in reclaiming ground and in building a breakwater in Panama Bay to cut off silt-bearing currents which were filling up the excavated channel. It has been built out about 2 miles by dumping from a trestle built for the purpose. One mile more remains to be built.

The slides in Culebra Cut have continued. The largest, called the Cucaracho slide, measures 2,700 feet along the cut, involving an area of 27 acres. During the year 1908–'09, 670,017 cubic yards were removed from this slide but it is estimated that

700,000 more are still in motion. Drainage seems to be ineffectual in these cases.

The original summit at Culebra Cut was 333 feet above the sea; it was lowered by the French to 157 feet and the lowest point at the summit is now 143 feet above sea level.

The lake section of the Central Division extends from Gamboa to Gatun. The Chagres River here crosses the line of the canal 23 times, forming a series of peninsulas. A portion of the channel 2,700 feet long, 500 feet wide at the bottom and 50 feet deep, was completed May 25, 1909 and the waters of the Chagres turned in. A total of 1,784,459 cubic yards were taken out, of which 1,350,308 were removed in 1908–'09. From the remainder of this division 2,625,283 cubic yards were excavated in 1908–'09.

To secure the necessary width and depth between Pedro Miguel and Miraflores on the Pacific Division 1,279,600 cubic yards of material, of which 63,600 are rock, must be excavated. The material still to be taken out between Miraflores and deep water is 13,000,900 cubic yards of loam and 1,725,000 cubic yards of rock. It has been decided to remove all rock between the locks and for 2 miles below the Miraflores locks, in the dry. This will leave 3,600,000 cubic yards of loam and 123,000 of rock to be removed by dredging and blasting.

The dredging fleet in Panama Bay for 1908–'09 consisted of one sea-going suction dredge, one 20 inch suction and pipe-line dredge, one 5 yard dipper dredge, and four French ladder dredges. They removed 8,475,931 cubic yards of material during the year. The channel is completed for about 5 miles from deep water in the Pacific.

The entire present steam-shovel equipment on the Isthmus consists of forty-eight 95-ton, forty-two 70-ton, ten 45-ton, and one 38-ton steam-shovels, or a total of one hundred and one steam-shovels.

Dry excavation for the first quarter of the fiscal year 1908–'09, (July 1 to October 1), cost 63 cents per cubic yard for direct charges and 12 cents per cubic yard for general administration, making a total of 75 cents. Dredging cost 9 cents per cubic yard for direct charges and 2 cents per cubic yard for general administration. The average cost per cubic yard for excavation was 40 cents for direct charges and 8 cents for general administration, making a total of 48 cents.

VIII. CONSTRUCTION OF THE LOCKS

Locks

As before stated there are to be 6 locks on the Panama Canal, 3 at Gatun, 1 at Pedro Miguel and 2 at Miraflores. All of these locks are arranged in duplicate, i.e., at any group of locks a vessel may ascend at one side of the middle wall, while another is descending at the other side. It is the intention that Pacific bound vessels use one side and Atlantic bound the other.

The middle wall is to extend 1,600 feet above the upper gates and below the lower gates as an approach wall against which vessels to be locked may lie while waiting for the gates to open. The side walls will not be as long, and will flare out at their ends. The lock chambers are to be 110 feet wide and 1,000 feet long and will pass vessels of 40 feet maximum draught in sea water. The upper lock in each flight is to be subdivided by additional gates into a 600 foot and a 400 foot lock so that water may not be needlessly wasted in passing small boats. These smaller subdivisions may be used until vessels of over 550 feet length require passage.

The lifts will average 28 feet, but will vary with changes in tide, lake level, and conditions of lockage. The diagram below shows the entire lock system at Gatun.

Fig. 2.—General Arrangement of the Locks, Valves and Gates at Gatun.

S.		V.,	Stoney	valve.
G.		V.,	Guard	valve.
E.	D.	P.,	Emergency dam	pier.
U.	G.	G.,	Upper guard	gate.
U.		G.,	Upper	gate.
M.		G.,	Middle	gate.
S.		G.,	Safety	gate.
L.	G.—U.	L.,	Lower gate, upper lock.	L.
L.	G.—I.	L.,	Lower gate, intermediate	lock.
L.	G.—L.	L.,	Lower gate, lower	lock.
L.	G.	G.,	Lower guard	gate.
Ch.,			Fender	chain.
Ga.,				Gauge.
L.,				Ladder.
St.,				Stairs.
Inc.,				Incline.
I.,				Intake.
O.,				Outlet.

In each side of the wall Between, there will be A and B— 3 cylindrical valves. C and D— 7 cylindrical valves. E and F— 10 cylindrical valves. G and H— 10 cylindrical valves.

Near the bottom of each wall will be a large culvert for passing water from the lakes into the upper chamber, and from chamber to chamber, and then out to the canal below the locks. The intakes (See Fig. 2) will be located at "I" and outlets at "O". The water enters and leaves the culverts through several small openings, the intakes being screened. The flow of water in the culverts is to be controlled by what is called the Stoney type of valves. These valves occur in pairs which are duplicated at each of the lifts so that if one pair is disabled the other set may be used while repairs are being made. On each side wall, at the middle gates in the upper lock there will be only one set of valves, but none in the middle wall. The flow between the culvert in the middle wall and the lock chamber is to be controlled by cylindrical valves capable of withstanding pressure on both sides. By using these valves water may be saved under certain conditions of lockage by cross-connecting the twin chambers through the middle wall.

In each chamber 11 laterals of 41 square feet cross-section will be led from the side wall culverts while at the middle culvert there will be 10 laterals having a minimum cross-section of 33 square feet. Each lateral will have five holes, each of 12 square feet area, opening up through the lock floor. The laterals leading from the middle wall culvert are to be controlled individually to provide for independent operation of the twin chambers.

The lake levels and the desired lock levels are to be maintained by large steel miter gates. At the upper and lower end of the upper chambers of all locks there will be two sets of these gates operated simultaneously so that a vessel entering the upper chamber will always have two pairs of gates between it and the lake. At the lower end of each flight, besides the regular gates there will be guard gates mitering in the opposite direction. They are intended primarily for holding back the water in the canal below, when the lock above is unwatered for repairs but may be operated during lockages purely as a safeguard.

As a protection to the gates heavy fender chains are to be stretched across the locks at critical places. They are designed by suitable retarding devices to bring a slowly moving vessel to rest before it can strike the gate. While the gates below are being opened the chains drop into recesses in the walls and across the floor.

Near the upper end of the locks and 200 feet above the uppermost gate, an emergency dam of the swing bridge type will be provided to be used in case of accident to the upper gates.

The following precautions against accident are to be observed:

First. All vessels must stop some distance from the gates.

Second. The lock operators here take the vessel in charge and control its passage through the locks.

Third. If a vessel breaks away from the operators or fails to stop at the proper place, it comes against the heavy chains stretched across the locks and is either brought to a full stop or is greatly retarded.

Fourth. In case a chain breaks, the vessel has two sets of gates to break, if at the upper level, where an accident would be most serious. Should all these barriers fail the emergency dam can be swung into place in a very short time.

The floors of the Miraflores and Pedro Miguel locks will have 1 foot thickness of concrete on top of the rock as a wearing surface. At Gatun, however the rock is of a character susceptible to the weather. It has therefore been considered necessary, in constructing the floor here, to leave the rock above grade until just before the concrete is to be placed and then to scrape and wash the surface to be covered. The floor in the lower portion of the upper chamber is to be of concrete 3 feet thick. The rock here is considered thick enough to withstand the pressure from the water-bearing stratum below. Above the middle gate, however, this stratum is too thin, and a floor 13 feet thick of concrete is provided and anchored by rails set in holes and surrounded by concrete.

The main floor level will be about 2 feet below the sills, in order that small objects dropped from vessels may be passed without being struck.

The sills for the gates are designed as concrete arches in a horizontal plane, 31 feet thick throughout and of 100 feet radius at the extrados.

The filling system is designed so that, with all valves opened the chamber can be filled in 8 minutes, but to prevent possible damage to vessels in the lock the maximum rate will probably not be allowed to exceed 3 feet a minute which would correspond to less than 15 minutes for filling.

Most of the foregoing discussion is taken from the Engineering Record[32] of February 26, 1910.

There has been much criticism of the lock sites, but the engineers now in charge seem to have perfect confidence in their work.

During the fiscal year 1908–'09 the work of excavating for the Gatun locks was continued by steam shovels and one 20-inch suction dredge. Material excavated in the dry amounted to 933,546 cubic yards, and that in the wet to 479,950 cubic yards. It was decided to construct curtain walls to stop any underflow; these will extend across the lock under the sill of the emergency dam and downstream outside the walls to the intermediate gates. As an additional precaution to making the concrete floor 13 feet thick as before mentioned a system of sumps under the floor with telltales in the walls will be built.

The plant for the construction of the locks is practically installed and ready for work, it being operated entirely by electricity.

At the Pedro Miguel locks 715,726 cubic yards were removed in 1908–'09. One lock chamber was completed to grade, but 45,000 cubic yards remain for removal in the other one.

At Miraflores work was done the past year with steam shovels and one suction dredge. The total amount excavated was 1,147,527 cubic yards which is one-half of the total estimated quantity.

IX. CONSTRUCTION OF THE DAMS

The Gatun dam has aroused more adverse criticism than any other canal feature. Most startling statements have been made concerning it. Its history is worthy of notice. The first study of the Panama route under United States authority was made by an Isthmian Canal Commission of which Admiral Walker was chairman and Generals Hains and Ernst and Mr. Noble were members. With respect to the location of locks, the report of this commission said: "No location suitable for a dam exists in the Chagres River below Bohio". Hains and Ernst signed this report. In a paper read before the American Society of Civil Engineers on March 5, 1902, Mr. George S. Morison, a very distinguished American engineer, said: "All engineers who have examined the route of the Panama Canal agree that the neighborhood of Bohio is the only available location for a dam by which the summit level must be maintained".

Under authority of the President, by executive order dated June 24, 1905, a board of consulting engineers was appointed to consider the various plans proposed for the construction of a canal across the Isthmus. The minority of the board, as has been stated before, recommended a lock canal with a dam at Gatun. The majority of the board, 8 to 5, opposed the idea of a dam and locks at Gatun on two grounds: first, that the introduction of locks in a treatment of the question was objectionable from many points of view; and, second, that the maintenance of a summit by means of an earth dam of immense magnitude to control the flood waters of this river introduced an element of great danger since the dam, without sheet piling, was proposed to be founded on the alluvial-filled gorges of the Chagres River, where the depth at one point extended 258 feet below the level of the sea.

Of the minority above mentioned one member, Mr. Noble, was a member of the former Commission who had reported that Bohio was the lowest point on the Chagres where a dam was practicable.

The report was reviewed by the Isthmian Canal Commission which included among its members Major Harrod and Generals Hains and Ernst. They all indorsed the minority report, notwithstanding the fact that in March, 1905, Major [34] Harrod was opposed to any lock plan, and that his two associates had said in 1901 that no proper site for a dam existed below Bohio.

It is true that every consideration of the Panama Canal type by any unauthorized body rejected the idea of a dam at Gatun, and its indorsement is confined to a minority of the board of consulting engineers and to three members of the canal commission who had previously either been in favor of a sea-level canal or who had said, in effect, that Gatun was not a proper site for the dam.

The attitude of the majority of the board of consulting engineers upon this most important question is best shown by an extract from its report. "The United States Government is proposing to expend many millions of dollars for the construction of this great waterway which is to serve the commerce of the world for all time and the very existence of which would depend upon the permanent stability and unquestioned safety of all dams. The board is therefore of the opinion that the existence of such costly facilities for the world's commerce should not depend upon great reservoirs held by earth embankments resting literally upon mud foundations or those of even sand and gravel. The board is unqualifiedly of opinion that no such vast and doubtful experiment should be indulged in, but, on the contrary, that every work of whatever nature should be so designed and built as to include only those features which experience has demonstrated to be positively safe and efficient".

The remarkable diversity of statement in regard to this dam is shown by the following quotations.

Mr. Teller in a speech in the last session of Congress said in part, "Let me say a word or two about the great dam to be built at Gatun. We were told in the beginning that the engineers would find a foundation upon which they could build a safe dam.

The French Government declared they had found such a foundation; our own engineers declared they had found it. It turned out that they had struck some floating pieces of rock in the mud, and when they had gone down 287 feet they found the same conditions practically that they found in the first 50 feet. The place where it is proposed to construct this dirt dam, which will be half a mile wide and 135 feet high (now 115 feet), is a great swamp. No such dam has ever been built in the history of the world, and the engineers of the world, with few exceptions, have declared it cannot be built. The dam at 35 Gatun is to be built upon a foundation of doubtful safety, and there is not an engineer in the country who does not know that it is doubtful".

Lindon W. Bates, in his "Retrieval at Panama", says, "The utter indifference to real information as to existing conditions at Panama has been astounding. Despite, for instance, the private knowledge of the Commission in 1906 through their last 15 months that the bores in these Gatun gorges were flowing bores, not one additional test had been undertaken in them. In summary of foundation conditions one thing is certain. First and foremost and indispensibly there must be at the Isthmus, since the underground conditions have been revealed, the safe barring off of permeable strata under the crucial dam. This cannot be done at Gatun for the high dam".

On the other hand an editorial in the Engineering News of February 25, 1909, says, "We can testify from actual personal observation and study of the dam site and of the borings and pits that the Gatun dam will be as safe and permanent as any structure ever reared by man".

In the President's message of February 17, 1909 there is this statement, "As to the Gatun dam itself, they (the board of engineers) show that not only is the dam safe, but that on the whole the plan already adopted would make it needlessly high and strong, and accordingly they recommend that its height be reduced by 20 feet, which change I have accordingly directed".

In the Engineering News of April 1, 1909 is the following statement, "If a private corporation, not subject to the clamor of public criticism were confronted with the task of throwing a dam across the Chagres Valley at Gatun, they would build a structure which would be not more than one-fifth the size of that which is now being built there". Farther on in the same article a comparison of the Gatun dam with alluvial dams of India and the levees along the Mississippi is summed up with these words, "Compared with any and all of these the conditions for safe and permanent dam construction at Gatun may be considered ideal". Is it any wonder that people are confused and disgusted when they attempt to obtain the truth?

The length of the dam is to be 7,700 feet, but the natural surface reaches or exceeds the dam elevation in three places for about 700 feet in all. At the level of 21 feet above the sea it will be about 2,600 feet long in two sections, separated by Spillway Hill.

According to the engineer's report the dam will rest upon brown or blue clay and silt. Under the dam there are two geologic gorges, one 185 feet deep (below sea level) and the other 255 feet deep. These are filled with river alluvium and other deposits, consisting, according to official reports, of silt, soil, brown and blue clay, rotten wood, sand, and gravel — the most, if not all of it water bearing. The cross-sectional area of the shallower gorge is 205,000 square feet and of the deeper one 120,000 square feet.

(For profile, cross-section, and plan see the following page.)

The dam is to consist of two piles of rock 1,200 feet apart and carried up to 60 feet above mean tide with the space between them and up to 115 feet above sea-level filled by selected material deposited in place by the hydraulic process. A slip occurred at one of these rock toes during November, 1908, and caused considerable alarm throughout the country, so much, in fact, that the President sent W. H. Taft with a group of 7 noted engineers to investigate. They reported that "A full study of all the data and of the material, and of the plans that are proposed leaves no doubt in our minds as to the safe, tight, and durable character of the Gatun dam".

At the close of the fiscal year 1908–'09 three 20-inch suction dredges were depositing material over the area between the rock piles, and the fill had reached an average elevation of 16 feet above sea-level. A total of 2,501,372 cubic yards was placed in the dam during the year.

Excavation through the Spillway Hill was practically completed and 30,464 cubic yards of concrete laid. During the year 359,821 cubic yards of material were removed from Spillway hill by steam shovels and placed on the dam.

The original canal plans provided for a flight of two locks at La Boca, near the Pacific, and one at Pedro Miguel. Steps were taken to construct the former and trestles were built along the toes from which to dump material from Culebra Cut. The trestles failed after dumping began and material overlying the rock moved laterally, the movement continuing for two weeks in some places. After this result these dams were abandoned so that instead of locks at La Boca they will be built at Miraflores. Another reason for the change besides poor foundations is the military advantages of the latter over the former position.

Both the dams at Pedro Miguel and Miraflores will be constructed of two rock piles, the portion between being filled by hydraulic methods. Very little work has been done upon them.

FIG. 3.—PROFILE ON THE AXIS OF THE GATUN DAM SITE SHOWING UNDERLYING MATERIAL AS DETERMINED BY BORING.

(From Report of C. M. Saville, Assistant Engineer, August 29, 1908.)

FIG. 4.—Revised cross-section of Gatun Dam as recommended by Board of Consulting Engineers, February, 1909.

FIG. 5.—GENERAL PLAN OF GATUN DAM.

X. SANITATION

At Panama the seasons are divided into two well defined periods: the dry, or winter, and the wet, or summer seasons. By this occurrence of maximum moisture and maximum heat, the health conditions are made the worst possible.

The dry season includes the months of January, February, March and April, the rainy season the remainder of the year. During the dry season the average temperature at Colon for 6 years was 70.5° F, with a monthly maximum of 90.9° F, which came in January, and a monthly minimum of 68.4° in the same month. During the rainy season the maximum average temperature for any month occurred in October and was 91.9° F. The minimum was 66.9° F., for August. A record of 15 years at Colon shows a maximum rainfall of 154.9 inches and a mean of 130.2 inches. Four years' records at Panama show a maximum of 84.73 inches and an average of 66.8 inches. At Culebra the records for 3 years showed a maximum of 98.97 inches and a minimum of 64.25 inches.

The most common forms of disease on the Isthmus are due to fevers. According to good authority the most sickly period is September, October and November, during which time dysentery and a severe bilious fever are very common. Foreigners seldom acquire the immunity of the natives from local diseases. The Isthmus by various writers has been called, "The Grave of the European", "The Pest-House of the Tropics", and one author says that here truly "Life dies and death lives".

On account of the health conditions the labor question is greatly complicated. For this reason extreme care has been taken by the United States Government to do all in the power of science to make the zone a healthy locality. Sanitation expenses will average at least $2,000,000 per year. The work has been under the direct supervision of Colonel W. C. Gorgas. The war on the mosquito has been continual and unrelenting. For the first two months of the fiscal year 1908–'09, the work in the Canal Zone, consisted of the collection and disposal of garbage and night soil, the cutting of grass and brush, and sanitary drainage and oiling. In the terminal cities the work consists of inspection,[39] fumigation, grass cutting, surface drainage, and oiling undrained areas.

This department also has charge of the hospitals and of the quarantine. As far as possible all the sick are concentrated at Ancon.

Last year's records show an improvement over the preceding year. The total number of employees admitted to the hospitals and sick camps amounted to 46,194, representing 23.49 as the number of men sick daily as against 23.85 for the preceding year. The number of deaths was 530. According to these figures the Canal Zone is one of the healthiest communities in the world; but it must be remembered that the population there consists of men and women in the prime of life and that a number of the sick are returned to the United States before death overtakes them.

There were no cases of plague or yellow fever originating on the Isthmus during the year 1908–'09. The last case of yellow fever occurred in May, 1906.

A supply of perfectly healthful water has been secured by the construction of reservoir at different points of the Zone, and the Commission hotels and cottages have all the advantages of an excellent modern water system.

XI. SOCIAL LIFE

Those who have endeavored to better the standard of social life at Panama have met with difficulties always connected with an enterprise of the character and magnitude of the great Canal. It is surprising what has been accomplished. Questionable amusements there are, but that is to be expected among such an assemblage of men. Nevertheless, the conditions of living there are gradually approaching what we find in the average community in the United States.

There is a well organized school system in the Canal Zone. Twelve schools are maintained for white children and seventeen for colored children. The highest monthly enrollment was 675 whites and

1,417 colored pupils. There is a superintendent of schools and assistant supervisor of primary grades.

Two high schools are in operation, one at Culebra and one at Cristobal. Children at other points in the Zone requiring high school instruction are given free transportation over the railroad by the Commission. Instruction is given in algebra, geometry, physical geography, general history, botany, English, German, French, Spanish, and Latin. There were but 25 children who took high school work in 1908–'09.

In addition to the transportation given high school pupils, transportation is given to children in towns where no white schools are maintained. Last year children were also carried by wagon from Balboa to Ancon, as were high school pupils from Empire and Culebra. A boat and ferryman were employed in two cases.

Quarters are furnished free to all the men, married and unmarried. Roosevelt, upon his return from Panama said the wives of the employees seemed satisfied with their home life and surroundings. The houses are excellent considering the conditions.

Employees purchase all necessary supplies from government commissaries at about the same prices as are current in the United States. On every workday a refrigerator car runs from Colon to Panama and delivers to the various villages all orders previously placed for supplies such as ice, meat, vegetables and fruit. Payment is made by the use of coupons, their values being deducted from the employee's[41] salary.

Employees are allowed free medical, surgical, and hospital attendance, including medicines and food while in the hospital.

Employees with salaries fixed on an annual or monthly basis receive no pay for overtime work but if their health requires it, will be granted a leave of 6 weeks absence or less during the year with full pay. Those who are paid by the hour do, of course, receive pay for overtime work.

A number of suitable church buildings has been erected by the Commission. They are two-story buildings, the upper floors being fitted up as lodge rooms and the first floor for religious purposes. Practically every religious denomination is now represented on the Isthmus by the chaplains employed by the Commission.

Roosevelt stated after his visit to the Zone that "It is imperatively necessary to provide ample recreation and amusement if the men are to be kept well and healthy." To this end four clubhouses have been completed at Culebra, Empire, Gorgona, and Cristobal and several more are contemplated. The four are alike in design, and consist of a front building of two stories connected with a rear building of one story. The front part is 135 feet by 45 feet, and contains a social parlor, a card room, a billiard and writing room on the first floor and an assembly hall on the second floor. The rear building, 100 feet by 28 feet, contains a double bowling alley, a gymnasium, shower baths, and over a hundred single lockers. The Commission, assisted by the Young Men's Christian Association, manages these buildings. Besides furnishing a library of 787 volumes to each of these buildings provision is made for the delivery of 100 weekly and monthly periodicals.

Last year 1908–'09, 2,140 employees availed themselves of regular membership privileges. The membership rate is 10 dollars per year. The fact that 56,835 games in bowling took place during the year shows the extensive use made of these buildings.

There are various athletic organizations on the Isthmus. Gymnasium activities have consisted mostly of basket ball and indoor baseball. Field sports are sometimes held on moonlight nights and holidays. An athletic park has been built near Cristobal.

During the year there were 81 performances given by lyceum and vaudeville[42] talent from the United States, with an attendance of 18,225. Chess, checker, glee, minstrel, dramatic, and orchestra clubs have been successfully maintained.

"These associations have held a vital relation to the canal construction in promoting contentment among employees, furnishing healthful amusement, effecting greater permanency of the force, and in elevating the standards of living".

XII. ECONOMIC IMPORTANCE

The economic importance of the Panama Canal is a fruitful topic for discussion. Some authorities think that a large share of the world's commerce will naturally and immediately use this new path between the oceans; but the general opinion of those best fitted to decide is that the canal will not be a paying investment, at least for the first years of its operation. As a German paper puts it, "Nobody thinks of remunerativeness any more. The fruits of the enterprise consist in indirect profits; they must be looked for in the military-political field and in the promotion of American commerce. In this lies the center of gravity of the situation".

From a commercial standpoint the canal will be of little or no advantage to Europe for the way to the whole of eastern Asia and Australia, inclusive of New Zealand via the Suez Canal will remain much nearer. For Europe, then, the only saving is in traffic with the west coast of America. In commerce with western South America England occupies first place, and is followed by Germany, the United States and France, in the order named. It is to be noted that vessels trading with the southern portion of the west coast of South America will prefer to go around Cape Horn rather than pay the tolls through the Panama Canal.

The greatest commercial advantage comes to the eastern ports of the United States, namely 9,531 nautical miles between New York and San Francisco, so that New York on this route gains 2,889 miles more, for example, than Hamburg, Germany. The main fact, however, is that this saving is so large on the route from New York to Eastern Asia and Australia that it changes the present disadvantage of New York into an advantage when compared with many European ports. From Hamburg to Hongkong, via Suez, the distance is 10,542 miles; from New York to Hongkong, via Suez, it is 11,655 miles. The Panama Canal will give nothing to Hamburg but a saving of 1,820 miles to New York so that the distance will be 707 miles less than from Hamburg. In routes to the more northern ports of eastern Asia, as well as to those of eastern Australia, the gain of New York is still greater. From Hamburg via Suez to Melbourne is 12,367 miles; from New York 12,500 miles. Via Panama, however, the distance from New York is only 10,427 miles, so that New York will be about 2,000 miles nearer than Hamburg. In many cases therefore the Panama Canal will give New York a decided advantage over European ports.

There are other than commercial reasons for building the canal. The effect which it will have upon the tropical districts of the west is worth considering. An author on "Social Evolution" in describing this region said that there are only two words which adequately represent the conditions of this country, "anarchy and bankruptcy", and he suggests removing the anarchy by the substitution of strong and righteous government. Can any one doubt that the construction of an international waterway through the Isthmus will tend to improve administration in the American tropics?

GENERAL MAP
OF THE
CANAL ZONE
AND THE
PANAMA CANAL

(left)

(middle)

(right)

Transcriber's Notes

Transcriber modified the original cover and added a map to it, taken from the original book.

The modifications as well as the original are in the Public Domain.

Punctuation and spelling were made consistent when a predominant preference was found in this book; otherwise they were not changed.

The original text was typed, not printed. Consequently, there were more typographical errors than would normally be found in a book, and Transcribers corrected most of them without noting the individual corrections here.

Ambiguous hyphens at the ends of lines were retained; occurrences of inconsistent hyphenation have not been changed.

Transcriber segmented the map at the end of the book into three larger parts for readability, in addition to retaining an image of the original.

"Maratime" was printed that way, twice; "Maritime" did not occur in this book.

Page 3: "concensus" was printed that way.

Page 15: "built on the lock canal" was printed as "built on the sea-level canal", but "sea-level" was crossed out by hand and replaced by what appears to be "Loc". Given the context and name of the chapter, Transcribers decided it was intended to be "lock".

**ISBN-13:
978-1981153992**

**ISBN-10:
1981153993**

Made in the USA
Middletown, DE
14 March 2025